Dream Time
TALES

PhP

PETER HADDOCK PUBLISHING

Contents

The Wise Woman of the Woods

nce upon a long ago, when the world was filled with wonder and many magical things happened, there lived a poor mother and her three children, Gretchen, Hans and Kay. The mother loved her children very much. But she was poor, and it was hard to find enough to eat. The family lived in a little wooden house on the edge of a great wood, and earned a few pennies by gathering and selling firewood.

One evening when Hans was collecting firewood in the woods, he heard a strange voice that sounded like crackling leaves.

"There's no gold in sticks," said the voice.

Hans turned around and saw an old woman standing behind him. She wore a long-hooded cloak and her face was as brown and wrinkled as a shrivelled apple, but her eyes were bright and twinkly.

"Who are you?" asked Hans.

"I am the Wise Woman of the Woods," she said, "and if you will carry out a task for me, I will give you a purse full of gold."

Hans agreed at once, thinking that the task might be to chop some wood or mend a leaking roof.

"Follow me," said the old woman. She led him deep into the wood, far beyond any place he had visited before. At last they came to a small clearing in the trees, and in the middle of the clearing was the old woman's home. It was a higgledy piggledy little house that looked as if it had grown there. But stranger still, the clearing was filled with all the animals of the woods. Hans stopped and stared. He could see foxes, bears, hares, stags, wild boars and wolves.

"Don't be afraid of the animals," said the Wise Woman of the Woods. "They are all my friends, and they need your help."

"What do I have to do?" asked Hans.

"Each night," said the old woman, "the King of Elfland and his hunters leave the underworld and come hunting in my woods. They kill many of the

animals and carry them away to eat them in the Elf King's banqueting hall. I will turn you into a wild boar and the elven hunters will chase you. If you are fast and run all night without being caught, then return here at sunrise to claim your gold. But if the King of Elfland catches you, at the touch of his hand you will become human and woe betide you then!" Hans was afraid. He had not expected such a hard task. But then he thought how pleased his mother would be to see a purse filled with gold, so he agreed to the bargain.

The Wise Woman of the Woods touched his head with a rowan wand and whispered some magic words. Hans felt his nose growing longer and longer, until it was a snout with tusks. Bristles grew from his back and his hands and feet became trotters. He was a boar!

"Run now," said the old woman. "The moon is rising above the woods and I can hear the hunters' horns."

Hans bolted into the dark wood. He was stronger and faster than he had ever been and it felt wonderful. But then the King of Elfland and his hunters came crashing through the trees like the wild winter wind. Their horses gleamed with a ghostly light and the riders struck fear into Hans's heart. He ran away through the undergrowth, zig-zagging this way and that to avoid the arrows and spears.

Hans ran all night long, charging through the dark woods to escape the hunters. But, just before dawn, his strength ebbed away and the hunters threw their nets over him. The Elf King leapt down from his horse and grabbed Hans by his bristly ears. At once the boy became human again.

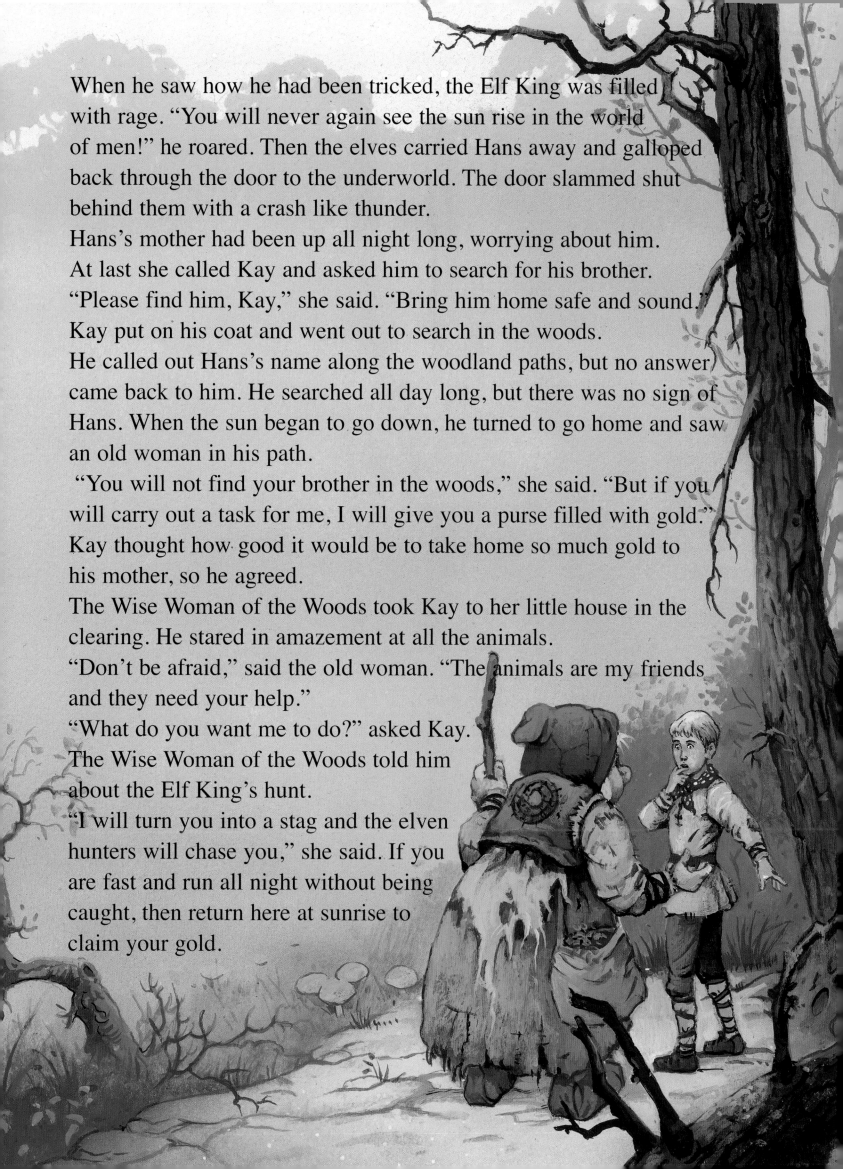

When he saw how he had been tricked, the Elf King was filled
with rage. "You will never again see the sun rise in the world
of men!" he roared. Then the elves carried Hans away and galloped
back through the door to the underworld. The door slammed shut
behind them with a crash like thunder.

Hans's mother had been up all night long, worrying about him.
At last she called Kay and asked him to search for his brother.
"Please find him, Kay," she said. "Bring him home safe and sound."
Kay put on his coat and went out to search in the woods.

He called out Hans's name along the woodland paths, but no answer
came back to him. He searched all day long, but there was no sign of
Hans. When the sun began to go down, he turned to go home and saw
an old woman in his path.

"You will not find your brother in the woods," she said. "But if you
will carry out a task for me, I will give you a purse filled with gold."
Kay thought how good it would be to take home so much gold to
his mother, so he agreed.

The Wise Woman of the Woods took Kay to her little house in the
clearing. He stared in amazement at all the animals.

"Don't be afraid," said the old woman. "The animals are my friends
and they need your help."

"What do you want me to do?" asked Kay.
The Wise Woman of the Woods told him
about the Elf King's hunt.

"I will turn you into a stag and the elven
hunters will chase you," she said. If you
are fast and run all night without being
caught, then return here at sunrise to
claim your gold.

But if the King of Elfland catches you, at the touch of his hand you will become human and woe betide you then!"

Kay was scared, but he agreed. The Wise Woman of the Woods touched his head with a rowan wand and whispered the magic words. Kay felt great antlers springing from his forehead and he dropped onto all fours. He was a stag!

"Run! The moon is rising and the hunters are coming!" cried the old woman. Kay bounded away through the moonlit trees. Just like his brother, Kay ran all night long, but just before daybreak his strength failed and he stumbled.

The hunters caught him and the Elf King leapt upon his back in triumph. But when the King touched him, Kay became human again. Tricked for a second time, the Elf King was even angrier than he had been with Hans. He and his hunters carried Kay off into the underworld and the door slammed shut behind them with a crash like thunder.

When Kay didn't come home, his mother wept. Her daughter Gretchen came to stand by her side.

"Don't cry, Mother," said Gretchen. "I'll find my brothers and bring them home safe and sound."

Gretchen searched all day. But though she looked up and down a hundred woodland pathways, she never saw a glimpse of Hans or Kay.

When the sun began to set, Gretchen turned sadly for home.

"You won't find your brothers in this wood," said a crackly old voice. Gretchen turned and saw the Wise Woman of the Woods standing on the pathway.

"Do you know where my brothers are?" she asked.

"Do a task for me, and I will tell you and give you a purse filled with gold into the bargain," said the Wise Woman of the Woods. Gretchen agreed at once.

The little house, surrounded by woodland creatures, surprised her just as it had amazed her brothers.

"Every night the King of Elfland and his hunters come hunting in my forest," said the Wise Woman of the Woods sadly. "They kill my friends the animals and carry them away for the Elf King's banquet."

"What do you want me to do?" Gretchen asked.

I will turn you into a hare and the elven hunters will chase you," said the old woman. "If you are fast and run all night without being caught, then return here at sunrise.

But if the King of Elfland catches you, at the touch of his hand you will become human and woe betide you then!"

Gretchen was a brave girl and she wanted to find her brothers. She agreed, and the old woman touched her head with a rowan wand and whispered the magic words. Gretchen felt her legs become shorter and stronger. Her nose began to twitch and her ears grew long and furry.

"Run now, for the moon is rising and I can hear the hunters coming!" cried the Wise Woman of the Woods.

In a heartbeat Gretchen was up and away. She was swift and silent, and she darted through the wood like a shadow. But the King of Elfland had eyes as sharp as knives and he saw Gretchen in a moment. The chase began. Past oak and elm, through bracken and briars, Gretchen ran all night long. But finally her strength failed and she was exhausted. She glanced around her as she ran and saw a hollow tree stump. Quickly she ran inside it and crouched down low in the darkness.

The King of Elfland searched high and low, but he could not find the little hare. When day began to break he knew that he had failed. Gretchen saw him open the secret door into the underworld. She watched the hunters gallop inside and the door close fast behind them. Then she ran back to the Wise Woman of the Woods.

"You are a clever child," said the old woman. She touched Gretchen lightly with her wand and the girl became human again.

"Where are my brothers?" she asked at once.

"The King of Elfland has carried them away," said the Wise Woman of the Woods. "By now they will have forgotten you, their mother and even their own names. How you will rescue them I can't say, for I do not know where the secret entrance to the underworld is."

But Gretchen knew. At the end of the day she went to the secret entrance to Elfland and, as soon as she heard the sound of the hunter's horns under the ground, she hid behind a tree. The door opened and the Elf King came charging out with his hunters. Before the door could close up again, Gretchen crept inside.

She was in a long passageway. The underworld was filled with a strange light that came from the rocks and the air was cool. Gretchen made her way down the passage until she came to two huge doors. She slowly reached out to touch them, and they flew open. Inside was a grand banqueting hall. It had a high ceiling and tall pillars of silver and gold, carved with twisting vines and leaves. Among the leaves were flowers made of diamonds, emeralds, sapphires and rubies.

The banqueting table was laid ready for a feast, with wine and fruit. The Elf King was at that moment hunting for meat in the woods. Gretchen looked around in wonder and then gave a cry of delight. At the far end of the long table were Hans and Kay.

"At last, I've found you!" she cried, running to them. But they did not look at her or smile. They sat still and quiet, as if they had been turned to stone. They had eaten the fruit and drunk the wine of Elfland, and had forgotten Gretchen and everything they had ever loved.

Gretchen's heart dropped. After all her bravery, she did not know any magic to break an enchantment. She put her arms around her brothers and wept. But as her tears fell upon their cheeks, Hans and Kay blinked and began to remember who they were. The enchantment was broken.

Suddenly they heard a crash like thunder. Day was dawning and the King of Elfland was coming back to the underworld. He burst in to the banqueting hall like a storm and roared with anger when he saw that his spell was broken. But Hans, Kay and Gretchen were protected by the love they shared and the Elf King's magic was powerless against them. They walked out of the hall and up through the passageway. The door opened to let them out and closed tight behind them.

The children returned to the Wise Woman of the Woods and showed her where to find the secret doorway into Elfland. She put a strong spell on it so that it could never open again. Then she gave Gretchen, Kay and Hans a purse of gold each. At last they went home to their mother in the little wooden house on the edge of the wood. She hugged and kissed them all, and they were never hungry again for the rest of their long lives.

Urishima and the Sea Princess

ong ago in Japan there was a young fisherman called Urishima. He was a very good fisherman indeed. Often he would catch more fish in one day than his friends would catch in a week. One bright morning when he was hauling his nets into the boat, Urishima saw a tiny turtle lying among the fishes. The creature looked up at him and its eyes were filled with sadness.

"Poor little turtle," he said, holding it in the palm of his hand. "Your kind can live for a thousand years, but you have come close to losing your life this morning."

Urishima gently put the turtle back in the sea. He expected it to swim away, but to his amazement it spoke to him.

"You have a kind heart," it said. "I am in your debt and would like to show my gratitude. Have you ever seen the palace of the Sea King?"

"No, but I have heard it is a beautiful sight," replied Urishima.

"Climb upon my back and I will take you there," said the turtle.

Urishima laughed. "How can such a little turtle carry a grown man?" he asked.

"That will not be a problem," said the turtle. As Urishima watched, it began to grow. It grew to be the biggest turtle that he had ever seen, easily large enough to carry two men. Urishima climbed eagerly onto its back and the next moment they were deep, deep under the waves.

Urishima found that he could breathe quite easily underwater. They passed over beautiful mountains and plains. Everything was softly lit by the sunlight that shone through the water.

At last they came to a marvellous palace that gleamed with silver and gold. It was encrusted with all kinds of jewels. They were greeted at the palace gates by a swordfish and a dolphin.

"The Sea King is away attending to important matters in a distant ocean," they said, "but the Sea Princess will see you."

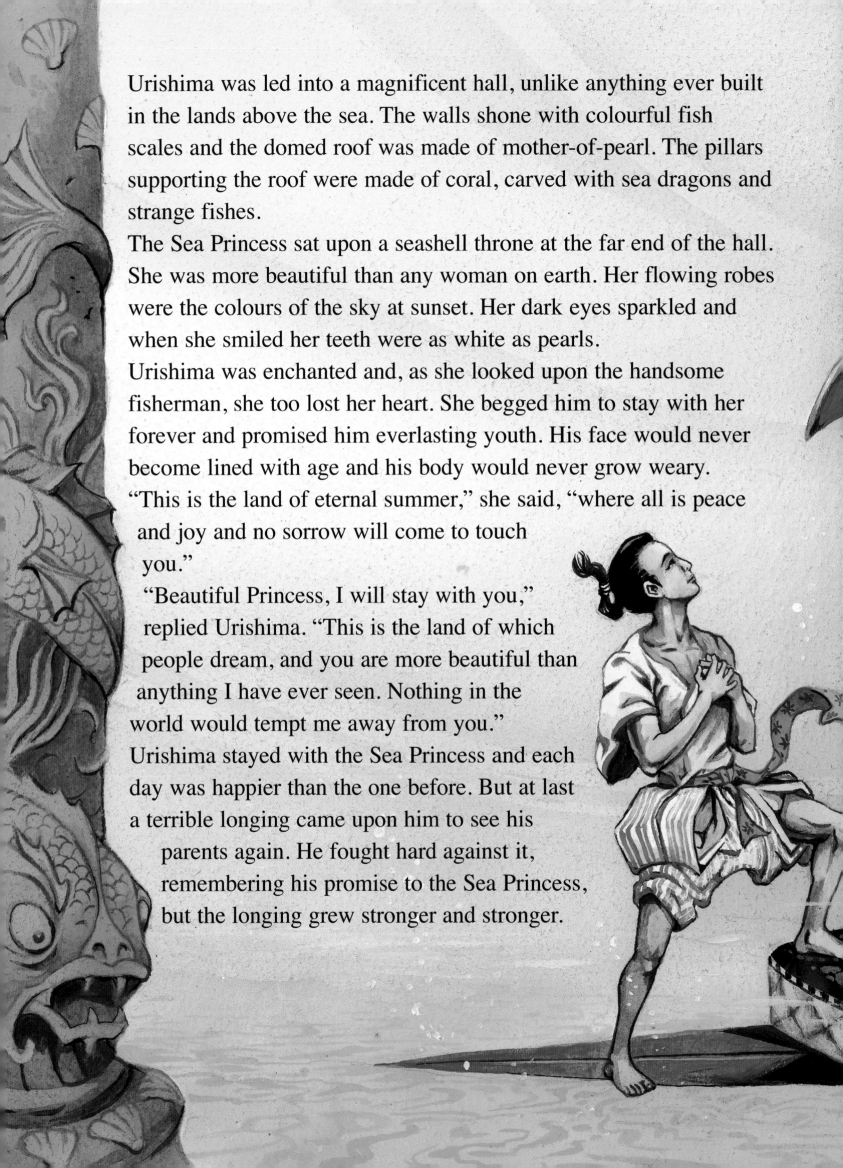

Urishima was led into a magnificent hall, unlike anything ever built in the lands above the sea. The walls shone with colourful fish scales and the domed roof was made of mother-of-pearl. The pillars supporting the roof were made of coral, carved with sea dragons and strange fishes.

The Sea Princess sat upon a seashell throne at the far end of the hall. She was more beautiful than any woman on earth. Her flowing robes were the colours of the sky at sunset. Her dark eyes sparkled and when she smiled her teeth were as white as pearls.

Urishima was enchanted and, as she looked upon the handsome fisherman, she too lost her heart. She begged him to stay with her forever and promised him everlasting youth. His face would never become lined with age and his body would never grow weary. "This is the land of eternal summer," she said, "where all is peace and joy and no sorrow will come to touch you."

"Beautiful Princess, I will stay with you," replied Urishima. "This is the land of which people dream, and you are more beautiful than anything I have ever seen. Nothing in the world would tempt me away from you."

Urishima stayed with the Sea Princess and each day was happier than the one before. But at last a terrible longing came upon him to see his parents again. He fought hard against it, remembering his promise to the Sea Princess, but the longing grew stronger and stronger.

The princess noticed his sadness and asked him what was wrong.

"Let me return to the surface world," he said. "I wish to visit my parents. They must think I am dead and be grieving for me. I will soon return and then I will stay by your side forever and a day."

"Urishima, my love," said the princess. "Your long hair is twisted around my heart. Please do not go."

"As soon as I have embraced my parents and put their minds at ease I will hurry back to you," said Urishima.

"So be it," sighed the princess. She gave him an exquisite tiny casket made of mother-of-pearl, with clasps of green jade. "Take this," she said, "in memory of me. But do not open it until you return to my side. If you do, then alas for you and I."

"I promise I will not open the casket until I am with you once more," said Urishima.

"Farewell then, my love," said the Sea Princess.

Urishima went to the palace gate, where he found the turtle waiting for him. He seated himself upon the turtle's back and was carried through the sea. Away from the beautiful palace, back over the mountains and plains, until at last they arrived on the beach near Urishima's home. The turtle promised to return for him that evening, and sank back under the waves.

Urishima ran to his house, eager to see his parents again. But when he reached it he found only a ruin, covered with moss. Where the vegetable garden had been, there were only weeds. No living soul was there.

"What is this?" cried Urishima. "Have I lost my mind?"

He rushed to the village to find his friends, but when he saw it he stopped in shock. When he left he had known every stone in the street

and every roof was familiar to him. But now the streets and houses
had changed and the people he saw were strangers.

Urishima pulled at the sleeve of a man passing by.

"Do you know of a fisherman in the village called Urishima?" he asked.

"I have never heard of him," answered the man as he hurried on his way.

Urishima returned to the beach, full of confusion and fear. There he
saw an old man quietly mending his nets.

"Do you know anything of Urishima the fisherman?" he asked.

"He was born and bred here and made his living as you do upon
the sea."

The old man looked at him, his eyes misting over as he searched
back through his memory. "There was a man by that name,"
he replied. "He drowned, and his body was never found.
It was very long ago. My grandfather told me the
story. It happened when he was a little boy."

Urishima felt fear grip his heart. "I am Urishima!" he cried. But the old man did not understand. He thought Urishima was mad. He abandoned his work and hobbled away as quickly as he was able.

Poor Urishima was filled with cold despair. Now he understood. The weeks that had seemed so short and passed so quickly in the Sea King's palace had been many years up here on the surface. His mother and father and everyone he knew had long since died.

Urishima thought of the little casket the Sea Princess had given him. He took it from his pocket and opened it, forgetting his promise to the princess. He hoped to find something from her that would console him, and for a moment he thought he heard her sweet voice calling his name. But there was nothing in the casket except a thin curl of purple smoke, which rose and coiled above his head then blew away across the sea.

As quickly as the smoke disappeared, Urishima's youth began to leave him. Deep wrinkles appeared on his face and his thick hair grew white and thin. Through dim and ancient eyes he saw the turtle swimming towards him, coming to take him back. He staggered forward, but it was too late. Age had come upon him and he fell down dead upon the sand, parted forever from the beautiful Sea Princess.

Adapted from a traditional Japanese fairy tale.

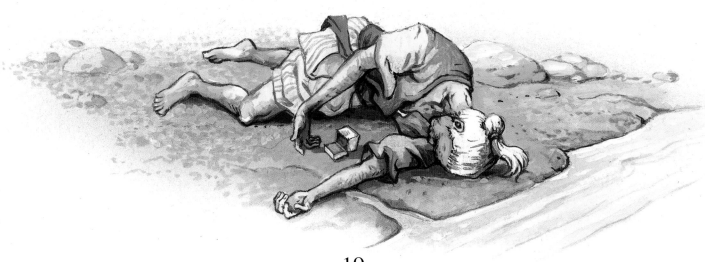

The Princess in the Tree

nce upon a time there was a Sultan who had a daughter named Parizade. She was clever and beautiful, but her heart was as cold as ice. Many princes came to woo her and when they saw her face they all fell deeply in love. But not one of them was good enough for her.

"Too short."

"Too tall."

"Too skinny."

"I want a suitor who will face fire and high water for me," she demanded. But there was no fire and high water to be faced, and there were no such suitors to be had. After the last prince left with a broken heart, the princess grew angry. "I will not waste another moment of my time on these foolish princes," she told her father. "Let no more of them through the palace gates." The Sultan always gave his daughter what she wanted. "I will put two enchanted stone guards at the entrance," he said. "If a suitor tries to enter, the stone guards will come to life and slay him."

The Sultan secretly hoped that Parizade would feel sorry for the princes and change her mind. But the princess's heart was hard and cold. "Good," she said. "I never want to look at another one of them."

No more suitors came to bother the princess, but she was still not happy. The truth was, Parizade was bored. Every day she sat in the library and read, or gazed out of the window at her father's kingdom. Every evening she walked through the palace gardens to the silver lake and watched the sun set over the purple mountains. And secretly she hoped that a brave suitor would ride over those mountains and prove himself worthy of her love.

One evening by the silver lake, the princess's dress brushed against a twisted tree. She did not apologise. It was only a tree, after all, and princesses don't talk to trees. However, this was a fairies' tree, and the fairies were enraged by Parizade's rudeness.

With a loud CRACK the tree opened up and a hundred fairies spilled out like a swarm of angry bees. They pinched the princess with their tiny hands, then dragged her into the tree and down to the underworld. Parizade tried to apologise, but it was too late. The fairies would not listen. They put her on a rock in the middle of a stormy lake and surrounded her with a ring of fire. Then they left her alone with the roar of the water and the crackle of the flames.

In the palace garden, the fairies joined tight together and used their magic to make themselves look like the princess. Then, in the twilight, they went through the gardens and into the palace.

The Sultan did not know that it wasn't his daughter. But as the days passed, he began to notice some strange things about Parizade. When she entered the room, he seemed to hear rustling leaves and branches creaking in the wind. He noticed once, when the princess was at the window, that her shadow looked almost like a twisted tree. At first the Sultan thought that he was imagining things. Then one day, when they were sitting in the library, he asked his daughter to fetch him a book. The fairies forgot themselves for a moment. The false princess stretched out her hand and her five pretty fingers transformed into five fairies, which flew away and quickly returned with the book.

The Sultan's eyes grew round with wonder, but he pretended not to have noticed anything. That night, just before Parizade went to her bedchamber, the Sultan crept silently to hide in her room. He watched the princess go to her window and open it wide. Then her body shimmered and turned into a hundred fairies. They flew out across the gardens and vanished into the tree by the silver lake.

The Sultan kept his knowledge secret from the fairies, but he sent a proclamation throughout the land. He would give half his kingdom to the man who could return the real Parizade to him. Then the poor Sultan sat back to wait for help to come.

Far away from the Sultan's palace, over the purple mountains, there was a young man named Khacan who was an apprentice to a wizard. The wizard had taught him magic and the secrets of ghosts, fairies and demons. When he heard about the lost princess, Khacan begged his master to let him try to rescue her.

"I think you are ready to face a challenge," said the wizard. He gave Khacan a magic sword and a horse with winged heels. "Go with a pure heart and fear no danger," he said.

Khacan rode for many days, stopping neither for food nor sleep until he arrived at the Sultan's palace. But as he passed through the gates, the stone guards came to life and stepped forward to bar his way. Khacan drew the magic sword and stood ready to fight, but at the first touch of the sword they crumbled into dust.

The Sultan greeted Khacan and led him to the fairy tree. "Rescue Parizade and I will make you a prince with a palace of your own," he promised.

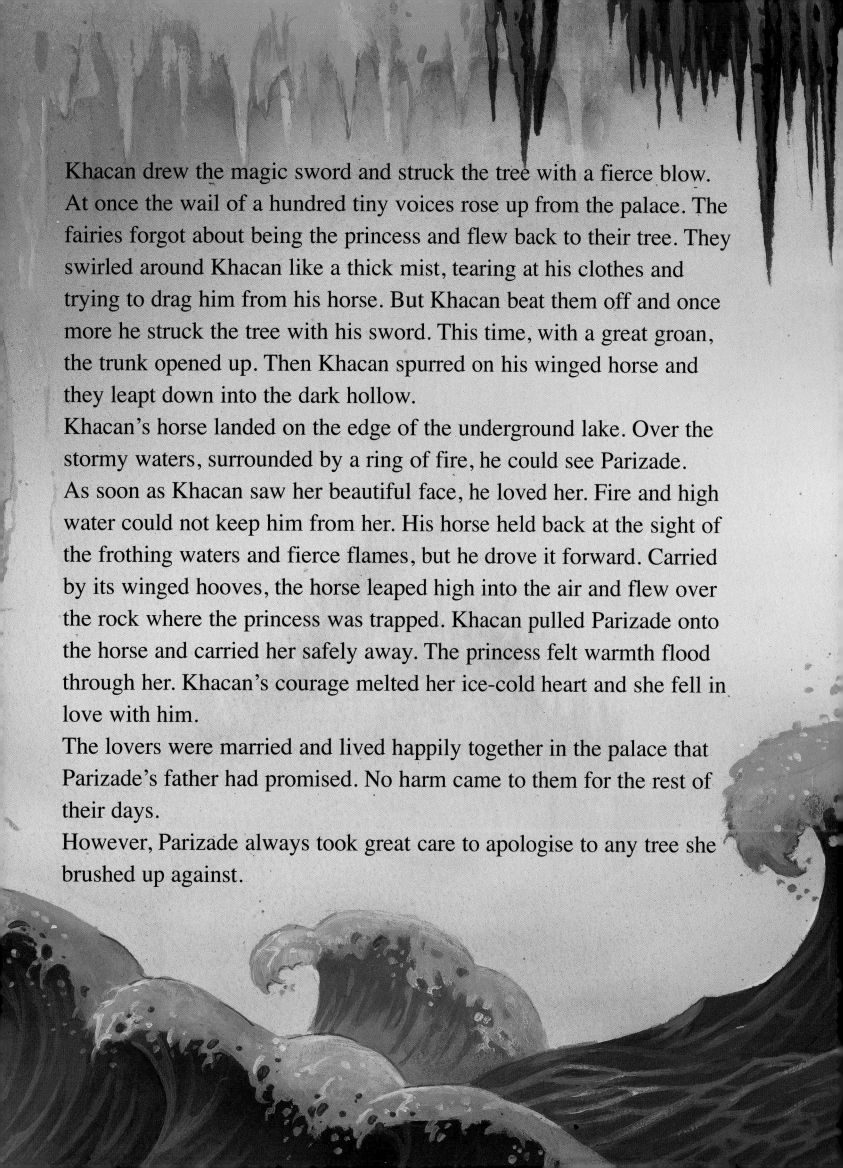

Khacan drew the magic sword and struck the tree with a fierce blow. At once the wail of a hundred tiny voices rose up from the palace. The fairies forgot about being the princess and flew back to their tree. They swirled around Khacan like a thick mist, tearing at his clothes and trying to drag him from his horse. But Khacan beat them off and once more he struck the tree with his sword. This time, with a great groan, the trunk opened up. Then Khacan spurred on his winged horse and they leapt down into the dark hollow.

Khacan's horse landed on the edge of the underground lake. Over the stormy waters, surrounded by a ring of fire, he could see Parizade. As soon as Khacan saw her beautiful face, he loved her. Fire and high water could not keep him from her. His horse held back at the sight of the frothing waters and fierce flames, but he drove it forward. Carried by its winged hooves, the horse leaped high into the air and flew over the rock where the princess was trapped. Khacan pulled Parizade onto the horse and carried her safely away. The princess felt warmth flood through her. Khacan's courage melted her ice-cold heart and she fell in love with him.

The lovers were married and lived happily together in the palace that Parizade's father had promised. No harm came to them for the rest of their days.

However, Parizade always took great care to apologise to any tree she brushed up against.

Fairy Hunters

Out from the wood where the screech owls call
The fairy hunters fly.
Hats of scarlet topped with feather,
Riding bats with wings of leather,
Over moorland spread with heather,
Under the moonlit sky.

With never a sound on the still night air
As soft as thistledown.
Over the trees on Blackberry Hill,
Close by the churchyard quiet and still,
Down by the river and watermill,
Where the water runs muddy and brown.

Armed with bee-sting, lance and bow
The fairy hunters fly.
Hunting moths of brown and red,
While the miller's in his bed.
Dreams rise up like baking bread
And no one will see them go by.

The Shepherdess and the Dwarf

Durinn was a rich and powerful lord of the underworld. He had endless majestic halls and treasure chambers and hosts of dwarves to rule over. Some dwarves mined silver, gold and precious stones. Others channelled the rivers of molten lava that flowed up from the earth's core. Most of the time, Durinn was happy in the underworld. However, once in a while, perhaps every hundred years or so, the fancy took him to visit the upperworld.

One fine morning Durinn went up to see how things were. It was so long since he had visited the upperworld that he had forgotten how beautiful it was. The warm summer breeze blew gently over the mossy grass. The wild flowers scented the air with their perfume and little white clouds moved lazily across the blue sky. Down in the valley, cattle grazed quietly in the patchwork of fields and cosy, thatched cottages nestled by the side of a sparkling river.

It was all very lovely and Durinn stood for a long time admiring the view. Then he saw some large boulders sitting on a cliff edge nearby. For fun, he put his shoulder to one of them and toppled it over, sending it crashing down onto the rocks below. It sounded like thunder. The people in the fields and cottage gardens looked up at the hills and wondered. Durinn laughed with pleasure.

The fresh air of the upperworld made the dwarf sleepy, and before long his head began to feel muzzy. He stretched himself out on the grass and went off to sleep.

Durinn was awoken by the sound of bleating. He opened his eyes and found himself surrounded by a flock of sheep. Their young shepherdess was staring at him curiously. She was a beautiful girl with golden hair and pink cheeks, and she made Durinn feel very confused. He had never allowed himself to be seen by a human but the girl was lovely, and he was smitten.

The shepherdess, whose name was Ida, wished the dwarf good morning and asked him if he was hungry. Dwarves are always hungry so Ida invited him to share her lunch, which she carried wrapped in a small headscarf. It was only bread and cheese, but in the open air it tasted delicious. When it was all eaten, Durinn was as much impressed by Ida's generosity as he was by her beauty.

"I am most grateful to you and wish to give you something in return," he said. "You are as pretty as a princess and every princess should have a palace."

He stamped his right foot three times. The earth split open and up sprang a gorgeous palace of white marble with tall towers and glittering golden domes. Before Ida could speak the dwarf clapped his hands three times and she found herself dressed in a gown of satin and silk, with a gold crown upon her head.

"This is a great deal more thanks than I would have expected for a bite of bread and cheese!" gasped Ida.

"Oh, we are not finished yet," chuckled the dwarf. He put two fingers between his lips and gave three shrill whistles. Again the earth split open and out rose a large barn, filled with thousands upon thousands of turnips.

The shepherdess was grateful and did not wish to offend the dwarf, but she was confused by this last gift.

"I am as fond of turnips as the next person," she said, "but surely you don't expect me to eat all those?"

"Indeed not, my pretty one," replied Durinn. He rummaged around inside his tunic and pulled out a slender rainbow-coloured wand. "Take this," he said. "Touch any of the turnips and it will become a servant to do your bidding."

With this, Durinn went back to the underworld. But Ida was so interested in touching turnips and creating an army of servants, she did not notice him go.

Durinn tried to carry on as before. He walked through the great stone halls with their high ceilings, inspected the work the dwarves were doing and ran his fingers through the jewels in his treasure chests. Everything was as it ought to be, but Durinn was not happy. He could not forget the pretty shepherdess.

At last, the dwarf decided to pay Ida a visit. He put on his finest clothes and his best hat (the one with a peacock feather in it). Then he pulled a bunch of red roses magically from a pool of molten lava and returned to the upperworld.

One of the many turnip servants who worked in the palace took Durinn to Princess Ida. She was fussing over herself in a mirror.

"I have come to ask you to marry me and be my bride in the underworld,"

Durinn blurted out, all in a rush to say it before he lost his nerve. Ida stopped looking at her reflection and stared down at him in disgust. Her pretty mouth twisted.

"A princess marry a dwarf!" she exclaimed with a cruel little laugh. "Quite ridiculous. Go away at once, back to your hole in the ground, before I have one of my servants throw you out of the window!"

Durinn was infuriated. "What an ungrateful girl you are!" he said angrily. "But I will teach you to be more polite to me. Where once you were pretty, now you will be ugly, and when you open your mouth toads will come hopping."

He snapped his fingers in the air three times. Ida at once became hideously ugly and when she opened her mouth to scream, out jumped slimy toads. Soon the floor was covered with them and the princess could hardly move.

"Stop it!" she spluttered. "I *will* marry you, only make me beautiful again and for heaven's sake get rid of the toads."

"Very well," agreed Durinn. He snapped his fingers in the air and things were exactly as they had been before. But a crafty look appeared on Ida's face.

"I can hardly wait to become your bride, my love," she said, "but we have no guests to attend the wedding and we must make a grand occasion of it. Wait – I have an idea! Let's make the wedding guests out of the turnips!"

"A wonderful idea!" smiled Durinn, who was happy again now he had got his way.

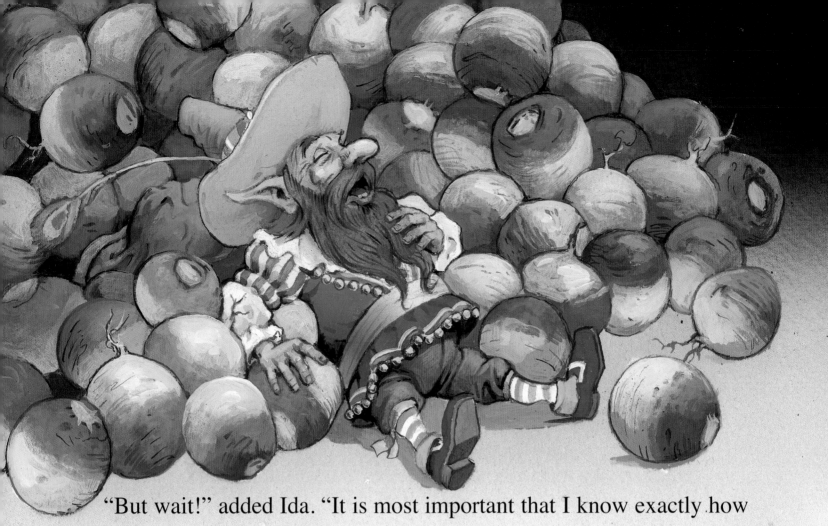

"But wait!" added Ida. "It is most important that I know exactly how many guests there will be. Go and count them for me would you please, my dearest?"

Wanting to make his beautiful princess happy, the dwarf ran off at once to the barn and began counting. However, the task proved to be much more difficult than he had expected. There were so many turnips! As he counted them he piled them up on one side of the barn, but the turnip mountain kept collapsing. Turnips rolled here, there and everywhere, so he had to keep starting again. But he kept going, telling himself that it was worth the effort to make Ida happy.

Durinn counted for hours, until at last he began to feel extremely weary. What with the fresh air of the upperworld and the endless counting, his head was swimming. He collapsed among the turnips and fell fast asleep.

As for Princess Ida, no sooner was the dwarf out of sight than she called in another suitor, who had been hiding in the next room. He was a fine prince, and Ida thought him much better than a silly dwarf who lived under the ground. She took her time prettifying herself in the mirror and packing a few of her most expensive possessions. Then she and her prince ate a delicious lunch served by the turnip servants.

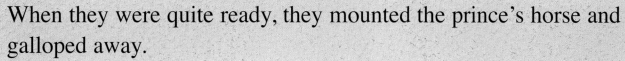

When they were quite ready, they mounted the prince's horse and galloped away.

However, as they rode past the barn, the pounding of the horse's hooves woke Durinn from his sleep. He was furious when he saw that he had been tricked. As the lovers rode away, he ran to a great boulder and began pushing it with all his might. It toppled slowly over and started to roll down the hill, gathering speed as it went.

Durinn leapt about in a frenzy of excitement, hoping that the runaways would be crushed. But the boulder bounced harmlessly over the prince and princess's heads and landed in the river with an almighty splash. The lovers rode on and were soon out of sight.

Durinn stamped his left foot three times and the earth split open. The white marble palace was swallowed up, gold domes and all, and the dwarf returned to the underworld, vowing never to trust a pretty face again. All that remained was a barn filled with old turnips.

Note: Durinn is a Viking dwarf name, meaning sleepy.

The Sea Fairies

eep in the cool, green water of the great ocean, a sea fairy named Crystal was busy at her work. She was an artist and made the most exquisite objects from the things she found around her. She collected coral and seashells and bits and bobs from sunken galleons and shaped them into statues and ornaments. She even made toys for the sea fairy children.

At present, Crystal was carving the frame of an oval mirror. It was the same size as her, which is about as long as your hand. She had carved a group of seahorses swimming through flowing ribbons of seaweed. The seahorses were made of mother-of-pearl, which shone with rainbow colours, and the seaweed was carved from pink and white coral. It was by far the most beautiful thing that Crystal had ever made and she was very proud of it. When she finished her work Crystal put her special signature to it – a tiny clamshell carved with the letter "C". She hid it in the coral seaweed. Then she put down her tools, left her workshop and went to gather seashells for future work.

From behind a rock, a couple of sea sprites watched Crystal leave with envy in their eyes. As soon as she was out of sight they rode up to the mirror on their seahorses.

"This will do very nicely," cackled one of the sprites. "The Sea King will pay well for it." They took Crystal's beautiful mirror and rode away, scattering a shoal of startled fish about them as they disappeared into the depths.

When she found that her mirror had been stolen, Crystal was heartbroken. Who could have taken her carving and how would she ever get it back?

The next day was market day and Crystal got ready to go with a heavy heart. She was sad that she did not have the mirror to take with her, as she knew that someone would have bought it. Crystal did not usually make much money from her carvings, but she knew that the mirror was very special.

Crystal had not gone far when she saw something that made her furious. A couple of sea sprites were tormenting an old crab, who was a very good friend of hers. They had tangled him up in ribbons of seaweed and were riding around on his back. The poor crab was snapping his pincers crossly, but he could not shake them off.

"Leave him alone, you bullies!" shouted Crystal, driving her clamshell cart at the sprites. They jeered at her but swam away when she got close. Crystal looked angry and the sprites were cowards at heart.

"Thank you, Crystal," said the old crab. "Those nasty sprites almost made me late. I was just on my way to visit the Sea King. I am going to show him my designs for the new palace."

"I'm sure he will be impressed," smiled Crystal. "I'm going to the market to sell some carvings."

"Then it's an important day for us both," replied the crab. "Goodbye, Crystal, I hope you sell lots of your lovely carvings."

The sea sprites had made Crystal late and by the time she arrived at the marketplace it was already very busy. The stalls were carefully laid out under the canopies of large seashells. One sea fairy was hammering away at a little bowl, about the size of a thimble. He had already gathered a crowd around him – sea fairies love to watch craftsmen at work. Crystal gave him a wave and began to set up her stall in a little crevice in the rocks. As she laid out her carvings she overheard a conversation between a catfish and a sea fairy who was selling baskets made from coloured seaweed.

"You don't honestly expect to sell any of this do you?" the catfish was saying. "It's all *very* ordinary. The fairies in the Mediterranean produce much better work."

"I just do the best I can," replied the sea fairy, shrugging his shoulders and rolling his eyes at Crystal. Catfish are grumblers. You might as

40

well ask the ocean not to be wet as ask a catfish to stop complaining. Crystal grinned and started to look for customers.

At the Sea King's palace the crab had arrived with his plans. He spread them out before the King, who was extremely pleased. As the King pored over the plans, the crab glanced around the room. One of his eyes was taken by a mirror with a beautiful carved frame.

"This is lovely," he said, scuttling over to the mirror and putting on his spectacles. "Dear me, how old I'm looking," he added, looking at his reflection. "But yes, as I thought, this frame is the work of my friend, Crystal."

"Who is Crystal?" enquired the King. The crab told the King about Crystal's wonderful work. "She sells all her carvings in the marketplace," he added. "But of course you must have met her when you bought the mirror."

"No," said the King. "The mirror was sold to me by a couple of sea sprites."

"A couple of scallywags, more like," snapped the crab. "Just look at this little shell in the coral seaweed. It has the letter "C" carved on it. That's Crystal's

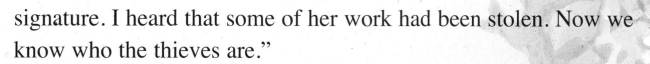

signature. I heard that some of her work had been stolen. Now we know who the thieves are."

The King tugged his beard thoughtfully. "I should like to meet Crystal," he said.

Back at the market, things were not going well for Crystal. She had sold a carved trinket box and a coral comb, but nothing more. The sea fairy watched the bright sunlight filtering down through the ocean and sighed. She would not be able to carry on with her work if no one bought it. Then she noticed a group of finely dressed fairies on seahorses coming towards her. As they came closer, Crystal realised that it was the Sea King and her friend the crab.

The Sea King's carriage drew up beside Crystal's stall and everyone in the marketplace came flocking around.

The King and the crab stepped down, and the crab introduced him to Crystal. Then the Sea King explained that he had Crystal's carved mirror, and gave her a little purse filled with pearls, in payment for it.

After he had looked around her stall, the King smiled at Crystal. "I am very impressed with your work," he said. "Would you consider becoming the Royal Carver?"

Crystal was overwhelmed. As soon as she was able to speak again, she happily accepted the offer.

And if they have not yet finished their work, and if you knew exactly where to look, you might find Crystal and her good friend the crab working together on the Sea King's new palace.

The Lane to Fairy Land

There's a lane that leads to Fairyland,
It's just a breath away,
You may find it in the evening time
Or at the break of day.
It's sometimes in the countryside
Where flowers scent the air.
It's sometimes in the city
Off a busy thoroughfare.
You will know it when you find it
By the shimmer all around,
By the piping fairy music
And the glitter on the ground.
Then glance over your shoulder
And bid this world farewell,
As the fairies fly to meet you
And you fall beneath their spell.
They will lead you into Fairyland
The pretty sights to see.
You will soon forget the folk you knew
And the things that used to be.
There's a lane that leads to Fairyland,
It takes a child to find.
It meanders down a hillside
Slipping quietly out of mind.

The Magic Music Box

nce upon a time there was a ballerina called Elvira. She was beautiful and talented and her dancing entranced everyone who watched her perform. Kings and queens fell over themselves to buy tickets to see her. Elvira was very famous, but she was also kind and gentle.

One evening, a prince came to watch the ballet in which Elvira was dancing. He arrived with the daughter of a rich merchant at his side. She had secret hopes that he might one day marry her, and then she would be even richer and able to call herself a princess.

The curtain rose and lights flooded the stage, which was designed as a moonlit wood. Then Elvira appeared, flitting between the trees. Her dancing was captivating and the prince fell in love with her at first sight. He could not take his eyes off her for the entire evening. The merchant's daughter was quick to notice this, but she hid her anger and the prince knew nothing of it. Very early the following morning, while the city was still sleeping, the merchant's daughter slipped through the quiet streets and went to see a sorceress. The room in which the sorceress sat was crowded with strange objects, half visible in the dim light. A black cat with glowing green eyes sat watching.

"How can I get rid of the ballerina?" asked the merchant's daughter. "I will give you more gold and silver than you can hold in your hat if you will help me."

The sorceress took a small, jewelled music box from inside her cloak and handed it to the merchant's daughter.

"Give this to the ballerina," she said. "But do not open it yourself or you will regret it."

Taking the music box, the merchant's daughter left the sorceress. As she went the cat followed close behind her. She stopped several times and did

49

her best to shoo it away, but the strange creature continued to slink along in her footsteps. She arrived home and went inside, closing the door as quickly as possible. But when she peeped out of the window, there was the cat, sitting quietly on her doorstep. She hurried to the scullery and returned with a pail of water. Opening the front door, she threw the water over the cat, which yowled and ran away. The merchant's daughter had made an enemy!

That evening, she disguised herself as a simple messenger girl and went to the theatre. The curtain had fallen on the performance and Elvira was about to change out of her costume. The merchant's daughter found the ballerina alone backstage.

"I have a present for you from a secret admirer," she said.

Elvira was surprised, but accepted the music box graciously.

"How beautiful it is," she said. She opened the lid of the little box and as she did so it began to play strange, tinkling music, haunting and insistent. Elvira started to dance, spinning round and round, faster and faster, unable to stop. At last the music ended and everything was strangely quiet. Then, frozen upon tiptoe, unable to move a muscle, the dancer saw the gigantic face of the merchant's daughter. Elvira was now just three inches tall, a tiny figure inside the magic music box. The merchant's daughter turned up her crimson mouth in a wicked smile and snapped the lid down.

Slipping quietly out of the theatre, she climbed into a waiting carriage. She was watched all the while by a pair of green eyes. The sorceress's cat had followed her and had seen everything. As the merchant's daughter rode away, the cat ran silently behind the carriage.

A little way out of the city, the carriage drew up by the side of a lake. The merchant's daughter got out and picked her way down to the water's edge.

"Let this be an end to you, Elvira!" she cried, flinging the music box from her. It spun through the air, flashed in the moonlight and fell with a splash into the depths of the lake. For a moment, the merchant's daughter watched the moonlit ripples of water widening. Then, with another wicked smile, she turned and left.

The next morning, the prince was sitting in his library, trying to read a book. But his mind was filled with thoughts of the beautiful ballerina. He had been to the theatre with a large bouquet of roses, but no one knew where Elvira was. She had simply disappeared.

The prince's thoughts were interrupted by the sorceress's cat, which leapt up from the garden outside and landed upon his windowsill. To his amazement it began to speak. When it told him what had happened to his beloved Elvira, he bridled his horse and set off for the lake, with the sorceress's cat perched on his shoulder like a parrot.

When they arrived at the lakeside, the prince stared down into the deep, murky water and was struck by the difficulty of the situation. "Never fear," said his companion. "I am a sorceress's cat and I know more than a thing or two about magic. Take one of those three bulrushes over there and break it."

The prince plucked one of the three bulrushes from the reed bed and broke it, and out sprang an emerald-green frog.

"Jump into the lake and bring us the little music box that you will find there," commanded the cat.

The frog got ready to jump but at that moment a heron flew down from a tree and greedily snapped it up. The prince was horrified, but the sorceress's cat just shrugged. "No matter," it said. "Break the second bulrush."

Once again, the prince did what the cat told him. The second bulrush snapped and out leapt a bright scarlet frog.

"Jump into the lake and bring us the little music box that you will find there," repeated the cat.

The turquoise frog jumped into the water and swam down into the depths. But out of the murk came an enormous pike and swallowed it in one gulp.

After waiting for an hour or more at the lakeside, the prince and the cat realised that something must have happened to the turquoise frog.

"No matter," said the cat. "Break the third bulrush."

The prince was beginning to lose faith in the cat, but he picked the bulrush and broke it. As it snapped, he felt a strange tingling sensation and in a flash he was transformed into a dazzling sapphire-blue frog. He did not need to be told what to do! He leapt into the dark lake and swam down into the icy cold water, deeper and deeper. There was little light and the prince was very much afraid of what monsters might be lurking in the gloom. For a long time he searched blindly in the dark, groping in the mud with his froggy fingers. Then at last he found it – the magic music box.

The prince grasped the music box and struggled back up to the surface. He placed the box on the mossy bank and, undoing the clasp, carefully opened the lid. The music began to play and the enchanted ballerina started to spin. As the frog and the cat watched, the tiny figure grew and grew until finally, there stood Elvira, as large as life. She stooped down and gently picked up the frog. Holding it in the palm of her hand, she kissed it lightly on the head and it once again became the prince, very happy but with rather wet clothes!

Elvira fell in love at once with the brave prince who had gone to such lengths and depths to rescue her. They were soon married and lived happily to the end of their days, always keeping a place of honour at their table for the sorceress's cat.

As for the merchant's daughter, she was never seen again. It is a mystery what happened to her.

However, the magic music box lies once more at the bottom of the lake!